This Cullercoats

work from
six village
writers

Carol Clewlow
Kitty Fitzgerald
Harry Gallagher
Peter Mortimer
Pauline Plummer
Josephine Scott

First published 2019 by IRON Press
5 Marden Terrace
Cullercoats
North Shields
NE30 4PD
tel +44(0)191 2531901
ironpress@xlnmail.com
www.ironpress.co.uk

ISBN 978-1-9997636-2-6
Printed by Imprint Digital

© Individual work, the authors 2019
© This book, IRON Press 2019

Cover design Brian Grogan
Book design Brian Grogan and Peter Mortimer

Typeset in Georgia 10pt
IRON Press books are distributed by
NBN International
and represented by Inpress Ltd
Churchill House, 12 Mosley Street,
Newcastle upon Tyne, NE1 1DE
tel: +44(0)191 2308104
www.inpressbooks.co.uk

This Cullercoats

What's Inside

First Word   6

Carol Clewlow   9
When I First Noticed it

Kitty Fitzgerald   19
The Tragedy of William Pearson

Harry Gallagher   29
Poems

Peter Mortimer   41
The Tallest Person Ever in Cullercoats

Pauline Plummer   51
A Symphony for Cullercoats (Poem)

Josephine Scott   59
Poems

First Word

CULLERCOATS HAS LONG BEEN ASSOCIATED WITH visual artists, attracting a whole host of painters over the years. At the end of the 19th century, this small and windy fishing village on the striking North East coast was the home of a thriving artistic colony and described as 'little Bohemia by the sea'.

The famous American artist Winslow Homer lived here for two years, a period which had a deep effect on his own style of water colours. You can find his name on a blue plaque on the newish and unstimulating seafront block of flats, Winslow Court and two plays have been written about his time here. There's also a blue plaque in St.Oswin's Avenue to artist John Falconer Slater. The 19th century saw several artists colonies spring up, though Cullercoats tended to attract more artists from its own region than others in this country, such as Newlyn or Staithes.

It was fairly recently that it struck me how many working writers the village now houses. For a place this size you might expect maybe a couple of published authors, but Cullercoats has six. Yet none of them is native to the place. All arrived and all stayed. This in itself tells us something.

It might be fun, I thought, to see if each of these six writers (whose numbers, I hasten to add, include myself) could respond to the challenge of writing either new short stories or new poems informed by living in the village of Cullercoats itself.

Our writers are equally divided, three poets, three prose writers and the approaches differ widely. Kitty Fitzgerald pens a darkly fatalistic tale of love misunderstood set in the aftermath of World War II; Carol Clewlow, the other novelist in the six, creates a modern day story that takes a sideways look at possibly the most important problem facing humankind, whereas my own prose contribution is a mythical explanation for a village structure whose origins have long puzzled me.

Pauline Plummer has created a single lyrical Cullercoats poem that observes the modern village, warts and all while Harry Gallagher and Josephine Scott both find poetic inspiration in the past and present life of the village and the natural elements that make up our community. How pleasing that none of these writers can be accused of being in any way twee, emphasising perhaps that individual and distinctive though Cullercoats is and very much attractive to visitors, it is far too gutsy ever to be considered twee. The village always has its sleeves rolled up, despite it recently becoming a centre for café culture.

This new café trend might of course partly explain its current richness of writers. Other professional writers live close by; the renowned crime novelist Ann Cleeves is just over the border in Whitley Bay as is the playwright and novelist Steve Chambers. There are others nearby too and poetry events attracting bardic aspirants take place regularly on the Marden Estate in the Sandpiper pub.

But this collection was specifically for Cullercoats-based authors whose work has already been published by reputable publishing houses. Plus which responding creatively to Cullercoats is a different matter for those who live here than for those who don't. Both are valid, but this book's concern is with the former.

I am delighted just how well the Cullercoats authors responded. Not only is it quality writing but they all met their deadline! I hope you find something worthwhile in these pages. The collection is meant as a celebration of the creative spirit and how, when challenged that spirit can find all manner of inspiration in what lies all around it day-to-day. Writers do not always have to trek to the other side of the planet.

My own aspiration is simple – that this book takes its own humble place in the rich cultural history of Cullercoats village.

Peter Mortimer

Carol Clewlow

When I First Noticed It

Carol Clewlow has lived in Cullercoats for 26 years after migrating from North Shields Fish Quay. She has written any number of novels, and published five. These include A *Woman's Guide to Adultery, Keeping the Faith* and *Not Married Not Bothered*. She is a founder member of *Operating Theatre* whose work is designed to change the way people think about health and well being and for whom she writes plays. Unhealthily addicted to the notion of hope over experience she is now working on another novel.

When I First Noticed It

FUNNILY ENOUGH IT WASN'T THE SUMMER ITSELF when I first noticed it. I mean, OK, yes it had been hot. God yes, it was hot that summer. Waking up every day to it, the clear blue sky and the sun cracking the heavens. Used to it now of course, but then. Just like a proper summer, the way I looked at it. The sort the Wilsons at 86 got every April, dicking off to their place in Spain.

Showing off the pictures in October.

'Oh look this is the terrace. And here's our favourite beach.'

Hah! Couldn't sell it in the end.

Lost a packet on it.

I never liked the Wilsons.

And OK yes, so London was melting. Rails buckling, tarmac melting. All that stuff. Everyday on the news. Bankers keeling over in the city. Like we cared.

But, no, it wasn't the summer when I realised.

It was October. End of October. Almost November. And it was late. Past nine. I'd gone out for my walk. I did that most nights. Along the sea front. A clear night with a moon and a silver strip across the sea. One of those big white moons like a Catholic wafer. Brought up a Catholic. Not that you'd know. And then comes this wind. That's the point. The wind. Strong enough to struggle against. And yet. And yet...

Because that's when I realised. About the wind.

It was warm.

The wind was warm.

October nearly November. Nine o'clock at night and it was balmy. I had to scrabble for the word. Because we'd never needed it up here. Just one more thing that belonged down South. Sitting out of an evening down there, outside in a bar or in friend's back garden. Glass of wine in your hand knowing you'd never be doing this at home.

And now here it was.

Balmy.

I hadn't been expecting it. I don't think anyone had. They'd never mentioned it on the forecast. Now I think they didn't know either. Didn't know any more than we did what was happening.

I'd been dreading the winter that was the thing. Every year, older I got, come the end of the summer, I'd think, Can I stand it? Another winter. Truth to tell I'd begun to think maybe not. There's moments you know. Don't tell me we don't all think it, when you wonder. Why bother? The cold. The wind.

Oh yea. The wind.

That other wind.

You have to be my age to remember that wind. Biting we'd call it. Wasn't enough. The word. Not fierce enough. Cut right through you, that wind. That's what we'd say. And that's what it felt like. A knife. Slicing straight through, front to back. Like it was personal, that was the point. Like it had seen you come out your front door and now was of a mind to make you miserable.

Funny thing, I could yearn for a blast of it now. Just to feel it, fresh and sharp in my face. Straight in from the Steppes, we'd say. Fresh in from Siberia.

Siberia. Hah! There's a thing.

They say you can't buy a dog kennel in Omsk now.

Mind you. Who'd have thought we'd have ended up on the nation's Most Wanted List.

Look. Here. Another one. Through the door.

Most days I get one.

Come in person too. Bold as brass. Cash in hand some of them.

This one, wide boy, pulls out a wadge of it.

''Ere and now. Ere and now. Cash in your 'ot little 'and.'

Cockney of course.

'Forget it,' I said. 'Only way I'm coming out of here is in a box.'

'Well, that can be arranged,' he says.
Cheeky bastard.
Sob stories. They're the worst. Claiming they want it for their granny burning up in Bromley.
Appealing to me.
'Granny to granny,' one of them said.
'I'm not a bloody granny,' I said.
They always assume.
There's plenty giving in of course. With that sort of cash washing around. Pushed into it some of them. I know for a fact poor old Alison at 43 didn't want to go. One small fall, and the kids had her up and out and into the old folks home before you could say hairline fracture.
Guy who bought it got the ones on either side as well. Knocked them all through.
Planning permission?
These days?
Don't make me laugh.
Built on the top too. Two more floors and a roof garden. Not the only one either. Buy the places for the old cottagey charm then stick these carbuncles on them. Conservatories. Balconies. Security gates. Totally out of keeping.
And now they're digging down as well. Latest thing. Designer kitchens, games rooms, home cinema in the basement.
Even a swimming pool in one of them.
Millionaire. Claimed he made his money in IT although drugs were mentioned.
Lived on his boat out in the bay while the work was going on. Big ugly thing. The boat. Although.
Mind you he came a cropper. Whole thing collapsed on him.
'I told him.' Pete the builder. Millionaire himself now although he denies it.
'I told him. There's tunnels all over man. The place is

honeycombed with them. Wouldn't listen.'

First pool party and the whole thing fell in on them. Found him under the iconic 19th century copper bath from two floors up. Hard not to indulge in a tad of that old schadenfreude. One persons's misery and all that.

Just an ugly shell now while the family argue it out.

Not my problem, luckily.

Family.

Don't have to worry about anyone trying to stick me in the old folks home or forge my signature to get hold of the place. And trust me, that happens. Everyone knows there was skulduggery over poor old Bill Cairns place. Some smart shit comes to the door, gets Bill to sign something he doesn't understand. Next thing there's a developer waving the paper in his face at the front door.

No-one's getting rid of me, I tell you. I love this place. Never wanted to be anywhere different.

In the old days, people would ask, 'Where you going for your holiday?' Never understood the question.

I'd say, 'Where would I want to go? I got the sea down the end of my street.'

'Course,' I'd say, 'The summer's not all they might be.'

Remember that? Hah!

Be careful what you wish for.

Anyway I never was good in the heat. I mean the serious heat. And now, of course, well, they're all burning up aren't they? All those places they used to go.

Which is why they all want to be up here.

And now, of course, with Parliament moving up. Couldn't take it anymore apparently. Falling asleep with the heat. Only surprised anyone noticed. And then, of course, half the City came too. Take the hover into town these days and you don't see a patch of green. Just roof after roof. I hate that.

Crazy when you think about it. All those years cherishing

that old North South divide chip on our shoulder. Now here they all are like refugees begging to be taken in. Not all as free with the cash as they once were either some of them. Little dockside pied a terres unsellable or waterlogged and the insurers they don't care. Course there's still plenty of places to go if you've got the money. Nuuk's the new in spot for the cognescenti according to the colour sups. You can pick up a nice little place there, all mod cons including the hot tub for under a million. Handy for watching the ice-cap melting.

None of which as I've said, affects me. I'm not aiming to move and not about to let anyone persuade me.

Still the time is coming. I know that. You can't live with a body for ninety plus years and not know when it's running down. Don't need the doc to tell me that. Even if I could find one.

Point is a decision needs to be made.

I thought about charities. Good causes. Refugees. Real ones. Night shelter. Food banks. Community law and medicine.

Then I thought about Raz.

Yea, I thought. Raz.

Just for the hell of it

Raz is like Tesco (yea some things don't change). He delivers. Comes on Thursdays. Not like the old days either. Brings them all ready rolled in a neat little packet.

My medicine.

All legal now of course.

Always stops for a chat, does Raz. Although mainly for his own benefit, so he can share with me the latest obscure strain of spirituality which he's discovered and reckons is going to change his life. Something to do with some ancient tribe living in the Outer Hebrides this time. Wiped out by the dinosaurs. I interrupted him in the middle of his blathering.

'I have to talk to you, Raz. Seriously.'

It was evening. We were sitting on the bench at the front of the house smoking.

'You know I'm on the way out. ' I didn't wait for any objections, although I probably wouldn't have got them. Another thing I like about Raz.

'Got no family. You know that.' I jerked my head back. 'So I'm thinking of leaving the place to you, Raz.'

Most people would have been surprised at this. But Raz has been smoking so long and so devotedly he's lost the habit of surprise. He just said, 'Cool,' perfectly calmly.

I said, 'Thing is Raz, there are conditions.'

I said, 'Can you promise me faithfully to fill it full of people like yourself not over scrupulous about their hygiene.' Another advantage of his long devotion to the habit is that it's made him entirely oblivious to insults.

I said, 'Can you promise to play loud music into the early hours, park a couple of clapped out old bangers permanently in the residents' spaces, have a beaten up old sofa and a couple of old mattresses rotting away out front.'

Raz doesn't do things in a hurry. He likes to think about stuff. Let his mind settle around it, so to speak.

So he pondered on this for a while, raising and lowering the joint tenderly to his lips. Pushing that ancient tribe from the Outer Hebrides to the side was my guess.

'Yea,' he said, finally, with a firm nod of his chin. 'I could do all that Lil.' Actually I'm Lillian but he always calls me Lil.

'Good,' I said. 'I'll make the arrangements.'

'Cool,' he said, it being the word that covers all occasions for Raz, and perfectly serviceable under the circumstances.

Business done, we sat there smoking quietly in the balmy velvety December night.

'Thing is, Lil,' he said, 'about Huddleston this tribe I was telling you about....'

Kitty Fitzgerald

The Tragedy of William Pearson

Kitty Fitzgerald was a modern nomad until she landed in Cullercoats. Born in Ireland, she arrived in England at the age of four after her father was taken to the UK by Churchill's post war commissions to help rebuild Britain. After that she lived in eighteen places before arriving in Cullercoats. Seduced by the singing sea and sands, the bay and the big sky she has settled here. Her writing includes five novels, short stories, plays for theatre and radio, film and poetry.

The Tragedy of William Pearson

WILLIAM PEARSON COULD BARELY remember his youth, shadowed as it was by the Second World War. The lines on his face reinforced his serious character, particularly the two deep valleys etched up from his eyebrows. He had not had much time for self-analysis either; the virus of the young in his opinion.

Just before war broke out, he was still living at home in Cullercoats and had recently finished his apprenticeship as a welder, taking special courses in underwater skills. Living near to the ship repair yards he thought it might come in handy. At first he paid little attention to the news and its predictions of a harsh war; he had love on his mind. On completion of his apprenticeship he proposed to his sweetheart, Cassie, on the north pier in Cullercoats Bay where they first kissed, aged 10 and 12.

As Hitler invaded Poland, war became inevitable and arguments began among William's companions in the Young Men's Discussion Group, attached to his church. Some of his group were pacifists and to William's knowledge, always had been. They refused to join up and got into furious rows with all the young lads eager to enlist. William often acted as arbitrator between rival groups, quoting chapter and verse of his religion at them: Thou shalt not kill (New Testament) An eye for an eye (Old Testament). Apart from Cassie, the teachings of the church were the only things William truly felt passionate about.

The autumn wedding took place, they moved into their flat in John Street and Cassie became the wife he'd always dreamed about. William was happy at home and at work and he thanked God for his good fortune. Apart from the war, the only thing that caused him concern was his next door neighbour, Harry Dobson who lived with his bedridden, invalid mother. Their two houses shared a common yard and outside toilet, making it difficult for the men to avoid each other.

Harry Dobson was a year younger than William and worked on the fishing boats out of Cullercoats Bay. He was always bringing things for Cassie, like fish and magazines from his mam and he often sat and had tea with her when William was out. Harry was also a pacifist and often tried to engage William in discussions on the subject. When instructions came for William to go and use his welding skills on weapons and military vehicles around the country, Harry tried to persuade him to 'object'. William lost his temper and threatened to hit the other man but Cassie insisted he apologise, which - with great reluctance - he eventually did.

The work was more interesting than William had expected; there was a sense of everyone pulling together and William was pleased to be part of the country's war effort. He went home almost every other weekend and filled the house and the church hall with tales about the black market, private drinking and gambling clubs, prostitution and more women working in heavy industry than ever before.

He knew that Harry Dobson visited with Cassie while he was away; she'd fed him fish that Harry gave her. But he bit back his annoyance and accepted that everyone needed a bit of human company in these dark times.

'He's been a real friend, always helping out,' Cassie regularly said.

But when William was home, Harry Dobson was rarely in evidence.

Cassie and his mam sent him messages to help his morale while he was away.

Dearest William, Hope you are safe. Your sisters, Emma

and Lily have been evacuated to Natland, near Kendal. If you're over that way, try and see them. Love, Mam x

May 1941. William, my love. You may have heard about the bomb destroying the public air raid shelter in the basement of Wilkinson Ltd in North Shields; it was on the radio news. I wanted to let you know that none of us were there. But 107 out of 193 men, women and children were killed. It was so dreadful. Harry was there for hours and hours helping out; I sat in with his mam and made a supper for us all. Can't wait to see you next week. Keep safe. All my love, Cassie x

Dearest William, the Germans launched terrible air raids on the newly commissioned aircraft carrier HMS Victorious which was due to leave the river Tyne and sail out past Cullercoats Bay. You'll never guess what some WRVS women are doing! They are combing dogs and collecting the dog hair, which can be woven into clothes!'

William my love, you'd be so proud of me; I've been helping the civil defence to keep a sea lookout on Bates Island! I cycle down and back with Harry and several times we've had to leave our bikes and run for shelter. We will defeat them, won't we William?

After reading this, William scrunched the letter into a tight ball, lit a Woodbine and set fire to the paper.

One weekend in June, 1942, William arrived home and was cheered by the familiar sights. Cullercoats Bay looked magnificent in the sharp light; he walked down to the water's edge and breathed in the salty air. He even convinced himself he heard the song of a goldfinch coming from a small group of bushes near Brown's Bay. That was until he heard the Luftwaffe flying down the coast and saw Harry Dobson shovelling a coal delivery into his and Cassie's shed. When he saw William, Dobson stopped, doffed his cap and went into his flat.

Inside William's house an extra special tea was laid out. Cassie was blooming; her eyes and hair glossy in the firelight.

She ran into his arms and kissed him several times.

'What is it pet?' he asked, 'You look like you've won the Pools.'

'Oh William, I'm so thrilled.'

'Well share it with me then.'

'Can't you guess?' she whispered.

He shook his head.

'A baby , we're having a baby.'

William was silent for a few seconds then he struck the table with his fist, making the sweet tea leap from the cup. It formed an undulating brown river across the lace tablecloth Cassie had crocheted. She jumped back in fright, smashing her own cup on the flagstones.

What's the matter William?'

'*His* bloody child, not mine!' he shouted. The skin on his temples stretched to cracking point as he pointed towards Harry Dobson's house.

Cassie backed away until she hit the wall.

'What? Why on earth would you think that?'

She stared at him in shock.

"You had your — your period when I was last home, so we couldn't make love…that's why.'

Cassie shook her head.

'William…I didn't know then but it wasn't a period it was a 'show' indicating I was pregnant.'

'Why didn't you write and tell me?'

'I wanted to see your face when I told you…oh William…the child is ours. I would never betray you.'

She moved towards him and he backed away.

'And just how can I ever be sure of that?'
'Don't you trust me?'
'I don't trust him.'
He stared at her, wild-eyed.
'Don't you understand, William? The show of blood, the nausea, the twinges of pain...that was all the beginning of *our* child.'
She tried to touch him but he flung her hand away.
'You're lying,' he said, with such venom that Cassie couldn't bear to look at him. She fled out of the kitchen and into the bedroom, sobbing.

William went to the church and prayed. By the time he returned home he'd convinced himself Cassie was an adulteress and the teachings of his church were very explicit on that. He packed his bag and when Cassie tried to stop him leaving he pushed her away.
'You've shamed me,' he shouted, 'and in our small community, soon everyone will know and laugh behind my back; I couldn't bear that.'
As he left the house, Dobson was sweeping both their yards. William dropped his bag, kicked the brush away from Dobson and swung several punches at his head. Dobson made no attempt to hit him back and in William's mind that was enough to confirm that Cassie had indeed betrayed him.

From that day on, William stayed well away from Tyneside and didn't respond to letters from Cassie or his family. Even after the war ended, he didn't go home. He told his parents and his sisters he wanted no mention of Cassie in their monthly letters but all of them tried to persuade him to return; to listen to what Cassie had to say; to see his beautiful son. He refused. As for the dozens of letters from Cassie which they forwarded to him...he threw them on the fire, unopened.

The years went by slowly and William never married. As usual, the church was his sanctuary and one day a letter arrived there for him. It was from the vicar at St George's church; Edward, the one who'd married him and Cassie:

Dear William, I think cutting Cassie and your son out of your life is a huge mistake. Please come home and let's try and make things right between you. She still loves you and your son needs you. Regards, Edward.

William was so angry at the priest's intervention on Cassie's side - because it went against church teachings - he threw it in a drawer and his heart grew more rigid.

A few months later he came across it again and saw the note written on the back of the letter:

We found this note ready for posting to you the day the Edward died.

Another knot formed in his chest: he had been unfair to Edward who had always supported him.

The anger at losing Cassie receded but William still didn't return to the north east coast until he was in his late sixties. He had no wish to claim his flat or see Cassie or any relatives who were still alive. Not yet, anyway. Instead he rented a room in Tynemouth and kept himself to himself.

But he walked: Long Sands; King Edward's Bay; around the priory and the pier; Freestone Point, The Black Middens and often he sat at Half Moon Skeers and thought he could hear someone calling him from beneath the waves, close to Old Man rock. Deep inside him the vicar's words kept repeating. Had he made a dreadful mistake?

That evening William went to the service at St George's. Several people stared at him, probably wondering if they knew him, but in William's jaundiced view, they were gossiping.

At the end of the service, the new vicar smiled and held

out his hand as he approached.

'William, thank you for your note; I'm so glad you came... come into the vicarage and have some tea.'

He guided William to the same room where William and Cassie had discussed their wedding ceremony and William's heartbeat suddenly accelerated. The vicar interrupted his thoughts with a tea tray, which he placed on the table. He poured tea for them and sat back in his chair but his eyes seemed to bore through to William's heart.

'Were you aware that Cassie, your wife had been very ill?'
William frowned.
'No, I...I haven't kept in touch...is she better now?'
The vicar shook his head.
'I'm afraid not, William...she died yesterday.'

An intense pain shot through William's body and ended with a hot stab to his chest. He dropped his mug, slid to the floor and passed out.

The vicar got him to the hospital in time to save his life but it was a major heart attack.

The hospital bell signalled visiting time. William turned awkwardly in his bed. All the friendly chatter of those coming to see the other patients disturbed him. His niece had called that morning and he expected nobody else. He gripped his safety bar and pulled himself round to face the wall, thankful to be at the end of a row.

A few seconds later, footsteps stopped at the end of his bed. William turned, expecting to see a sympathetic nurse. But what he saw almost finished him off: a man nearly identical to himself forty years previously. William blinked and thought he must be dying. When the man spoke, William didn't want to hear the words:

'Hello father.'

There was no doubt that this man was his and Cassie's

child. He had Cassie's eyes; and hair. He had William's mouth and hands. The misery of all the missing years, all the emotions kept under tight control, were almost too much for his weakened heart. His son pulled up a chair, took hold of William's hand and held it firmly. Neither of them spoke for almost twenty minutes; William's tears seemed endless but he gained some strength from his son, David's grip.

'Why did you do it?' David eventually asked.

William took a deep breath and blew it out slowly.

'Jealousy…Harry Dobson…he was always there…I thought…'

'You were so wrong. He was a good friend to mam and he was a homosexual; something a man kept quiet in those days.'

William sighed and slowly nodded his head.

That night, alone in his hospital bed, William raged against himself and the God that had allowed him to commit such a crime against Cassie and his son, David. He pounded the bed until he lost consciousness.

Harry Gallagher

Poems

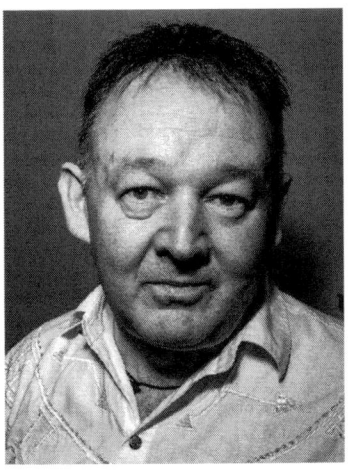

Harry Gallagher was born and raised in Middlesbrough, but escaped to Cullercoats some years ago, where the locals have been very tolerant thus far, despite his best efforts. Like many who float unthinking too close to the bay for a day out, he was captured by the tide's invisible magnet and couldn't now bear to leave. He is constantly fascinated to learn more about the village's history and can often be heard from afar, attempting to 'educate' disinterested strangers about salt pans and mines and fishwives' black bonnets. He is widely published and runs the north east stanza of The Poetry Society from the Crescent Club on the seafront.

Boatman

His beard is a mop for waves,
his good side a motor
which powered him on
through a force nine stroke.

He is in his element.

He lopes left into Rocket
where he rescues boats.
Another day, another bonnet,
another voyager kept afloat.

Brake pipes purged of salt,
he looks out for the drowning,
the all-at-sea. Winter is coming
and he will not be found wanting.

Where Hopes Holiday

In a world inconstant, mad,
this promontory perseveres,
a harbour where hopes holiday.

They come for a spot of r&r,
staying in a b&b of their choosing,
sleeping in the raw space
between warring bedfellows,
armed with olive branches
and second chances.

Sneaking out of the window
just before dawn's beaming face,
they stretch, weave slinky limbs
in and out of rusty railings.

Whizzing electric in the morning,
they buzz around telegraph poles,
sending applecheeked messages
about sunshine and showers
being two sides of the same coin.

Boatyard Stakeout, 16:30, 6 October 2018

Outside, fighter seagulls
clear airspace for bomber command
while the couple in the café
whistle low code across the table.

Hands joined at the controls
they draw lines on unseen maps,
whisper plans about rose cottages
and the moulding of a team
of little secret agents.

The couple in the café
will not be buffered by East winds
as they discuss the weather
and everything but.

Talking long-term on shortwave,
secret agents Livvy and Dave
have special forces on their side.

The Bombing Of St John's Church

Not the good Lord nor St John
were sitting on a cloud
when a fiery feather
tumbled through it from Heaven
and took a little boy
sending love letters to Christ,
toying with the keys
of a sleepy eventide organ.

Maybe they were snoozing,
omnipotence fatigue
closing their eyes
to the Daddy spared
by the doorway he stood in
to feel for wee pink fingers
and their splintered white keys,
their lovely song
smothered by brickdust.

Angel Of The Navtex

Viking, Forties, Cromarty, Forth,
Tyne, Dogger, Humber, Thames,
Fair Isle; the clicking of modems
echoes seawards from the North.

Steelfinger in air, reading the wind
for trepidatious trawlers.
Gan further oot or tie down wor haul?
Shirtsleeves an' bracers or full oilskins?

At a splash off fifty five degrees,
a printer whirrs in perfect time,
weaving threads through hungry brine
for those in peril on the seas.

The Very Temporary Industrialisation of Cullercoats Bay

Beside a church, beneath
a manicured field,
two hundred feet down
yawns a hidden hollow...

*'Tis her Ladyship's pleasure
that a new colliery
shall be sunk in the bounds
of Tinmothshire,
its shaft within sight of sea
at Caller Coates.*

*And as the sinking progresses
we shall require a pier
and of course a beacon
whose mast will fall
and take a man –
Mr Thomas Lorraine –
in a singular
act of spite.*

*And whilst we're about it
a grand wooden waggonway,
some fifteen yards wide
to weave a path to Whitley.*

A cosmic eye blinks...

Pier long gone, pit forgotten,
the ailing Newcastle opens its arms
and points sorry to the depths
of its cellars.

Wooden parallel lines,
already a wisp,
are ripped up in
an eyebrow's lift.

Their footnote rescued by children
who play games on a mine
and hopscotch between
the shadows of saltpans.

Cullercoats Bay – A Cautionary Tale

Don't come for a day
to Cullercoats Bay,
do yourself a favour
and steer well away
from the friendly locals,
from Bill's fish & chips,
from the sheer blue horizon
at the top of the cliffs.

Don't listen to the tales
that drift off the waves,
rumbling through the belly
of the smugglers' caves.
They'll trip you and trap you
until one awful day
you'll find yourself anchored
in Cullercoats Bay.

You'll end up as hooked
as a catch of the day,
boring folk with the history
of the old waggonway.
As you drone on about Marconi
watch them smile and back away.
You'll be halfway through
an unlovely oratory
all about the wonders
of the Dove Laboratory
when you come to your senses,

the daylight diminished,
the streets are all empty
and the metros have finished.

So don't come for the day
to Cullercoats Bay –
march away in your boots
before they put down roots
or you'll never get away
from Cullercoats Bay.

Peter Mortimer

The Tallest Person Ever in Cullercoats

Peter Mortimer has had a life of loss. First there was his virginity (in Nottingham) then his hair (many places) and later his faith in Notts County staying in the Football League. He has written more books and plays than you could throw a North Shields kipper at, yet inexplicably his mantlepiece stays unadorned by the Man Booker Prize trophy. He compares editing IRON Press and being artistic director of Cloud Nine Theatre to riding a bucking bronco and he's much too old for that kind of thing. Despite his occasional 25 year long tiffs with its institutions, Cullercoats remains in his soul.

MOST PEOPLE WHO LIVE IN OUR SEASIDE village are unaware who was the tallest person ever to live here. Or the fact that the person (that word will do for now) was exceptionally tall. How tall is that, you ask? 6ft 5ins? 6ft 6ins? 6ft 8ins? Taller even?

Stop guessing now, because you will not get it right. The tallest person ever to live in Cullercoats was 40ft tall. Yes, that's right, 40ft. And that person is buried right here in the village.

Take a walk along to the wonderful French Gothic church that is St George's. This sits above the cliff tops at the North End of Tynemouth Long Sands, overlooking the beach and the Beaconsfield open land. It's an impressive though not imposing presence, and at 60 metres high, towers above the rest of the skyline. This is three times the height of the Angel of the North and at least twice as high as any other building in the village.

As you journey south towards Tynemouth, St. George's is the village's final and dramatic statement.

The church soars so high above all else that it seems appropriate it houses the grave of someone who himself soared so high above everyone else. The person's name was - well, I'm not sure there was a name. No stonemason chiselled the details into the gravestone which is without any reference to who lies beneath. In fact Cullercoats made sure there was as little clue as possible to the identity and the grave itself was not built without some resistance and controversy.

You may well have seen the long horizontal blank slab and thought little about it. After all, why suspect a grave? One clue is that the church grounds do not boast a cemetery, nor any other graves. The slab, or the series of small connected slabs, lies in the grass area alongside and just south of the church itself.

I have met no-one (including the present incumbent Father Adrian Hughes) who has any idea as to the origin. The grave is very long, also narrow indicating that the person was not only unnaturally tall, but also very skinny. The height was not remotely to scale with the rest of the body, so although it had arms, legs, a torso and head, compared to a normal human being it looked rather odd. And why shouldn't it? Because it wasn't. A human being that is. Normal or otherwise.

What on earth, you might ask, is this creature doing, buried here in Cullercoats?

Firstly, a bit of advice. Don't even think of digging it up. I can tell you on good authority that anyone who even attempts such a thing is not long for this world. I happen to know that in every other instance (and there are not many) of a human attempting to dig up such a body, that human has been dead within minutes. How? Vaporised. Gone up in smoke as you might say. One minute there. The next, blown away on the wind. And possibly only a pair of shoelaces or glasses, or in one case an upper set of dentures to suggest the digger-up had ever existed.

So how does all this come about? If I said it was all to do with a temporal slip, would you be any the wiser? I thought not.

Firstly, let me start by saying (and bear with me) that though we humans know of only three dimensions, there are quite a few more. Thousands in fact. It's just that we are not aware of them.

We ask ourselves when did the universe begin and what was there before that? We ask ourselves how far away does it stretch and if it does have an end what happens if you keep going after that? There are no answers to these questions because they are not the right questions.

What are the right questions? We can't as yet know them, because we are limited to our three dimensions, but if I said an example of a relevant question might be 'How is yellow?' it might give you a clue. None of us, given our current capabilities, would know how to answer such a question.

In a multi-dimensional universe, there are an infinite number of 'times' travelling in parallel lines like railway tracks, but never touching. One time, one existence may be only a micro-second removed from another and another. All exist simultaneously and all are linked, but no single one can ever occupy the space taken by another.

Confused? Patience. Consider the words in this story. Each is an independent entity and can be read perfectly well in isolation. Yet the words are linked in such a way as to create a special pattern – ie the story you are reading. Consider the single isolated word (where we all live) as one reality or dimension. But consider the overall pattern, the coming together of those different words as the millions of realities that make up the universe itself. Not that we as individuals can ever be aware of that. All we have is our own single 'word', our own reality.

Put a word in the wrong place in a book and it will stick out like a sore thumb. The balance is upset. Same with all these different realities. Which normally doesn't matter because they're in the right place. But just occasionally they get misplaced, Part of one reality ends up in part of another. Then you're in trouble.

What has all this got to do with some lanky 40ft tall entity buried in the grounds of St. George's Church? And how come no-one seems to know about it?

Our tall stranger had come through what's known as a time/space slip. Beings do just occasionally get dislocated into another time channel. How? Who knows? But it does happen infrequently.

Remember, we are not talking here about travelling from one century to another. Each exists in its own time channel, neither before nor after any other, just as those parallel railtracks are all travelling simultaneously but destined never to meet. And each reality evolves independently. Which means they might take all different shapes and sizes. Such as a 40ft high human.

Just very occasionally there is a mishap (think of a word mistyped in a book,or the occasional wrongly sorted parcel at the post office). And we get a time/space slip. Normally the fault is automatically readjusted fairly quickly by the powers-that-be - we could discuss the powers-that-be but that would be a whole volume on its own. This rapid readjustment is why most spottings of so called 'aliens' are episodic. Few aliens are seen day-after-day in the same place. They are no sooner seen than gone again, back to their own dimension/reality. Only in sci-fi films and novels are aliens spotted over a longer period. This is a plot convenience. In real life, spottings tend to be isolated incidents.

But just very occasionally the system *does* fail and the misplaced entity *does* find itself stuck here for good. Let me give you two examples; The Loch Ness Monster and the Abominable Snowman. Each has been spotted through the centuries. Each is an example of a misplacement that the powers-that-be have been unable to rectify. Yet significantly each has the good sense to stay away from humans as much as possible, despite our attempts to track them down. Each knows just what the human race can do to other species – and the stranger the species, the more likely bad things will happen. So each spends its time in isolation - at the bottom of one of the deepest lakes in Europe or in a frozen wilderness.

Now we come to the crux of the matter. One other rare example of a creature being stuck outside its own time channel/dimension is here in Cullercoats. And in our small village anonymity is not as easy as it is in the frozen tundra;. Especially if you are 40ft tall.

Thus, having been stranded here by accident, the being calculated that its best chance was to attempt to befriend and integrate with the local populace. Like many small places, Cullercoats is close-knit, proud of its heritage but also often wary of incomers, especially 40ft incomers who do not immediately merge into the surroundings .

So when the creature popped up outside the Hudleston Arms (which later went on to become The Bay Hotel, which then went on controversially to be rebuilt as a block of flats called Winslow Court) the reception was far from welcoming.

If it had been able to speak English – or even Geordie - it might have helped. But it couldn't.

The noise when it opened its mouth (similar to a human mouth) was more a krrk-krrk sound followed by a loud roar. Words which in English meant 'Look, I'm really sorry, I didn't plan to be here at all and am merely a victim of circumstance,' came out as 'krrk-krrk, roar, roar, krrk'...

And because simply everything was different, the creature (though able to survive), was unsteady, forced to wave its arms as it stumbled around. Both the different speech and different behaviour were enough to generate fear among those who had gathered at a safe distance.

And then, unfortunately and entirely by accident, the creature stumbled backwards and collided with a small child. The child immediately began bawling and the creature attempted to soothe it. But its movements were awkward and it only made matters worse. The frightened child fled to the safety of its mother, bawling loudly. And though the creature tried to communicate, again the loud noise came out as 'krrk, roar, roar, roar, krrk!' And again, this made matters worse and what had been fear of the unknown turned to aggression towards it, as the humans interpreted the whole behaviour as being hostile.

'Drive the thing out! Drive it out!' This shout came from one villager who picked up a nearby stone and hurled it. And sometimes one small act, even an aggressive act can seem to give licence for others to act the same. A murmur spread through the crowd and now another man threw a stone at the creature.

'Yes, drive it out!' yelled this second man. The angry shouts increased. More stones were thrown, forcing the creature to stagger over the road, down the slipway and onto the beach.

By now the crowd had increased and with that dangerous sense of the mob, were baying for blood. There was nowhere for the creature to go except into the precarious sanctuary of a cave. In fact, the largest cave, for in truth it would not fit into any other.

And even in the largest cave it had to stoop and bend.

It was in this cave that the creature's life ended. Not immediately, not gloriously nor dramatically. Once inside the cave, the creature was scared to emerge. Just as the residents of the village were scared to enter those dark confines. Thus fear immobilised both parties and contact between both was nil.

The creature cowered and hid, stooped low in the back of the cave. The villagers gathered at the cave entrance armed with rough weapons ready to repel any attempts from it to emerge. As the tide came in and flooded into the cave the villagers retreated from the beach and up the slipway, taking up position again once the tide receded.

Yet each tide weakened the creature, rendered it more exposed and frozen, less able to comprehend or deal with the extremities of this world into which, through no fault of its own, it had stumbled.

A few of the villagers suggested entering the cave, but they were shouted down. On two occasions the creature itself half emerged, attempting to communicate with those gathered at the entrance, but its strange sounds and the cave's amplification were taken as more aggression and it was driven back.

And each cold, forbidding and relentless tide, its resistance grew less. Waves battered it, the cold water sapped at its very lifeblood until on the fourth tide, the creature slumped down at the rear of the cave and was consumed by the sea. Hunger had killed it, thirst, cold and exhaustion had killed it, fear had killed it. And ignorance had killed it.

For several months the body lay at the back of the cave. No-one knew what to do. Until a few villagers proposed that at least the dignity of a proper grave should be afforded this unlikely visitor. Others said the 'marauding' creature should simply be allowed to rot away in the cave as an example to others.

A compromise was eventually reached. A grave would be allowed but no identity was to be put upon it and there was to be no official record of the incident ever having taken place. Nor was the incident ever publically to be discussed.

Under cover of darkness, the body was carried out of the cave and laid to rest in the 40ft shallow grave that had been specially dug. On top of this was built the low brick base and marker slabs. There was no ceremony.

All of which was many years and many many lifetimes ago. Occasionally someone may remark upon the strangeness of this structure, but in the main it lies unnoticed, buffeted by the strong North East winds, an anonymous symbol of a forgotten yet extraordinary episode when Cullercoats was accidentally witness to a visit from a time/space dimension which was and remains beyond its comprehension.

Pauline Plummer

A Symphony for Cullercoats

Pauline Plummer (Hughes), an Irish/Welsh mixture from Liverpool, has lived in the North East since 1982. She brought up a family and taught creative writing at Northumbria University and the Open University; she now cooks a lot, runs book clubs, paints, has tried to learn Irish, travels as much as possible and belongs to pressure groups fighting for Justice and Peace, racial equality and the environment. She is working on a novel. Her latest poetry collection is *Bint* (Red Squirrel Press); her verse novella *From Here to Timbuktu* published by Smokestack; her short story collection *Dancing With a Stranger* by Red Squirrel. She is a founding editor of Mudfog Press. *Demon Straitening* (Poems) was published by IRON Press.

I - Opening sonata, Allegro
The sky is a glass of pink champagne
and the pale sea sips at the edge.

You're playing your tenor sax laughter
at dusk and our voices are singing
acapella in the wind.

The warm dough of your arm's around
my shoulders and gritty sand rubs between my toes.

I've got egg shells in my pockets.
You're not yet un-shackled, not yet banished,
not yet gone, not yet lost, not yet sectioned.

I've bought a cashmere coat before
I've earned my wages,
written your epitaph
before I've paid for the stone.

II Scherzo
In the nightclub of the sea
where swashbuckling voices roar
over the percussion of good-time girls
and the brush sweeps the skin of the snare
and the Aretha voice of the singer
lifts and falls to the climax of loss
or the roar of contempt, here now,
be right, be good and the drunks slurp
their sex on the beach while in the gents

the gigolo boys do a line
their heads fizzing in the flush and rush
of lacy froth.

III Adagio
Waves are rumpled, change colour
from brown to blue to grey.
The boat's engine thrums.

The wizened fisherman
in a lumberjack shirt pulls out
sheets of fishing net.

Seagulls overhead mew
as the boat cuts through silvery frills
to check on lobster pots.

Engines pause
as two boats stop to gossip.
Words skim the sulking waters.

The fisherman, rocking gently,
looks beyond the rocks and cliffs
at the solid symmetry of the town.

IV Allegro
Sleet slouches in over a pewter sea
that's shed astounding plastic tat.
Kelp, dulse and wrack
have been thrown by a maniac.

Here the wind plucks a drone

across frosted grass and snug terraces.
People's faces mushroom

out of dark coats. Children scream
and whirl in the playground
like seagulls starved by storms at sea.

Deep in the sand are the
splinters and grains of Roman,
Christian, Viking and Saxon clutter
and the remnants of coal and salt pans.

The cliffs wear ancient masks
over caves hiding secrets,
washed by the inscrutable tide.

V Staccato
They come out of the station at noon
the loud bare-chested men
their bare-chested dogs beside them
chains glinting in the sunlight
of an oven-baked summer.
Their razors of teeth
grin for a sign of disrespect.

The men's tattoos and bum cracks
are dark and inky. Their women scream
as if their mouths were crammed with toxic waste
as if the beach was their bedroom
If you pulled off their hardened shells
What unripe fruit would you find?
The sound of their despair is deafening.

Cigarette smoke hangs like gas
in the trenches. The men bayonet
the coal-speckled water
and detonate cans of Stella and
polystyrene containers of chips and kebabs.

At night rats will come for the waste.

VI Adagio
I walk towards a line of blue on the horizon
writing stories on the sand
examining the indent of a wing print
in the honeyed grains.

I remember women from other places
walking for miles, with babies
on their backs, bowls of smoked fish
balanced on their heads,
their future tied in a knot
in the hem of their lappas.

Sometimes it seems our souls
are ships in glass bottles,
ready to navigate by the stars,
if only the sails were unfurled.

VII Largamente
Escape from myself in the cold swell,
a sheet of shaken pale blue silk
or is it grey? A trick of the light.
All this space with the stars and planets
hidden behind the chiffon of sky.

Hear the cry of the sea and the earth
and the cry of the poor.
Listen to the last, the least, the lost.

A low boat pleats the waters
lights on its bulkheads.
Dusk is drawn in faint charcoal.
The rocks pulse with their stored heat.

The sun will leave a line of blood beyond
the houses to the west, built on land
hiding other dwellings of stone, clay and wattle, wood.

The cold water whips my skin.
The shock of it
like suddenly understanding something difficult,
that loving others is hard.

Josephine Scott

Poems

Josephine Scott was born in Northumberland, spent her childhood in Australia, and has lived in Cullercoats for over thirty years. She has two poetry collections; *Sparkle and Dance,* and *Rituals*, both published by Red Squirrel Press. Her third, *When Rain Becomes Memory* will be published in May 2020.

Anchor

Waves wash
    tear
      pull
        take
Wild
  rage-thrown
      forces
plunge me
  under

    You
    shelter
    seize

    raise me
    once more.

No 12 Bank Top

Late afternoon
they wait on The Bar
eyes set upon the sea
never wavering,
look for returning
rectangular sails,
fishing boats
making for shore.

I mix burnt sienna
with ultramarine
for leaden sky, add
carmine for a troubled tide,
churning its strength
against land
and absorbed
in the spirit of women,

whose time is spent
combing for bait,
backs stooped
hands busy rakes,
or mending nets
fingers calloused
and chapped
by coarse wet twine.

I sketch each woman
onto canvas, pick out
mussel-shell blue skirts
against the muted palette
of this wild place.
Fish flash silver,
heads and tails thrashing
as creels lift onto hips,
babies onto backs.
Life's weight
carried with determination.

Footnote: The artist Winslow Homer maintained a studio for eighteen months at No.12 Bank Top from spring 1881 until November 1882.

Syzygy

And just for that one day,
after the lunar eclipse,
when the moon pulled the tides
so low, we could walk between the piers
on coal streaked sand to look
for the glitter of sea glass.

Past curtains of seaweed
hanging from the sandstone walls,
below a colony of limpets
sheltering in worn cups,
stepping over coiled casts left by lugworms.

To the middle of the bay.
Our gaze drifting out to a lone
fisherman, silhouetted by the sinking sun,
standing on the mudstone outcrop
where fossils can be found.

Then turning towards the Bank Top,
I thought about all the years
I had known you, and the wasted time
in between, like the wide sea behind me,
and the comforting arms
of the breakwaters by my side.

The Beach is Desolate

Ice needles pit craters
attack steep cliffs.
I shelter in the Fairy Caves,

leave prints on washed sand,
run fingers over ancient letters
chiselled into rock,

PG   Henry   Cory
the *ache*
in fading *Rachel*.

An abandoned nest tumbles
out of a crevice,
a single feather lifts.

Storm clouds blur
the horizon,
ghost ships flicker.

Tide like liquid time
sneaks in
curling round the piers.

The Catch

Rounding Brown's Point
avoiding Nancies and Goaties
we line up the glow of beacons
ride waves into the bay.

Moisture clings jewelling
ganseys, each a suit of light;
salted winds frost chapped lips,
stiffen fingers.

A huddle of lasses
wait along the strandline
their chatter keen
as gutting knives.

There's silver in nets
a glint in every eye.

The Women
After the painting by John Charlton 1910

We women come, running along Simpson Street, shouting, knocking on doors and windows, clogs ringing on wet cobbles. A collier brig has floundered on rocks off Whitley Sands.

> Daybreak's beginning
> to New Year. The sky charcoal.
> Tempest raging.

With salt on tongues, shawls tightened across bodies, driven by wind we head to the Boat Field. Hands ready-roughened by course work, we grab the ropes, bend into the haul. The grass beneath our feet treacherous, we slip trying to get a foothold.

> A south easterly peppers
> each face with sleet.
> Nothing deters.

Hair blown into mouths, tangled skirts between rubbed-raw legs. All is a churning of bodies: men, women, six horses - flanks steaming - panting, breath catching. Silently chanting a litany of village fishermen yet to come home. Just over two miles, maybe 4000 footsteps heaving the lifeboat across land to launch off Brierdene. Gulls rise, their screeches drowned by breaking waves.

> Women's pounding hearts
> in each step of trodden ground
> are lights in the storm.

You Come Through Driving Rain

Wait for me
at the Watch House.

Look out
to elephant grey

waves
curling piers,

wind blasting
shingle to shore.

Oystercatchers
lift.

Gulls worry
a washed-up can.

I will follow
your footprints

along the sand.

Cullercoats

There is music in the soil

whispering in the sands

churning on the waves

echoing in the caves

sea shanties

folk

frantic rock tunes

endless skies

empty shells

scattered stones

washed up coal

mournful gulls

a foghorn's moan

scarred rocks

currents

swell

undertow

ebb and flow

pulling us home.

IRON Press is among the country's longest established independent literary publishers. The press began operations in 1973 with IRON Magazine which ran for 83 editions until 1997. Since 1975 we have also brought out a regular list of individual collections of poetry, fiction and drama plus various anthologies ranging from *Voices of Conscience, Limerick Nation, The Poetry of Perestroika, 100 Island Poems* and *Cold Iron, Ghost Stories from the 21st Century.*

The press is one of the leading independent publishers of haiku in the UK.
Since 2013 we have also run a regular IRON Press Festival round the harbour in our native Cullercoats. This book is launched at the fourth festival, *IRON OR,* in June 2019.

We are delighted to be a part of Inpress Ltd, which was set up by Arts Council England to support independent literary publishers. Go to our website (www.ironpress.co.uk) for full details of our titles and activities.